Cool Kids Have Manners

Author
Nathaniel Monk

Illustrated
Sameer Kassar

"Being kind is the best gift you can give your parents, siblings, and community"

Dedication

This book is dedicated to my beautiful wife Krista, our new angel on the way, and our cool kids Malachi, Evelyn, Moriah, and Knile.

As the story goes

The coolest kids in all the lands.
Were boys and girls from Mannerplan.

They searched the floor they moved her desk.
They found it there Mrs Brooks yelled Yes!

Another cool kid known as Charles
Helped elder neighbors mow their lawns

Cool kid Lake was washing plates
Her Mom stayed late at work today

When Mom came home and seen it clean
She told Lake thanks we are a team

Cool kid Joe had pride in school
He helped new students love it too

Cool kid Max saw Frankie cry
A bully pushed him from behind

Max ran over told him quit
That is not cool say sorry quick

Cool kid Laya laughed and screamed
Her sister won in hide and seek

New kid Joan walked into lunch
Hoping to sit down with someone

The parents stood and clapped together
We hope our kids have manners forever.

The End

About Author

Nathaniel Monk is a award winning songwriter, reknowned author, and the creative genius behind "Cool Kids Have Manners" series. His stories teach children the fun in being respectful at home, school, and within their community. Born in Brooklyn, NY and living many different places, he seen the growing problem parents and teachers faced getting children to be nice to all people and reduce bullying. Deciding to show support and do something about it, he wrote Cool Kids Have Manners.

Made in the USA
Coppell, TX
17 November 2021

65926007R00017